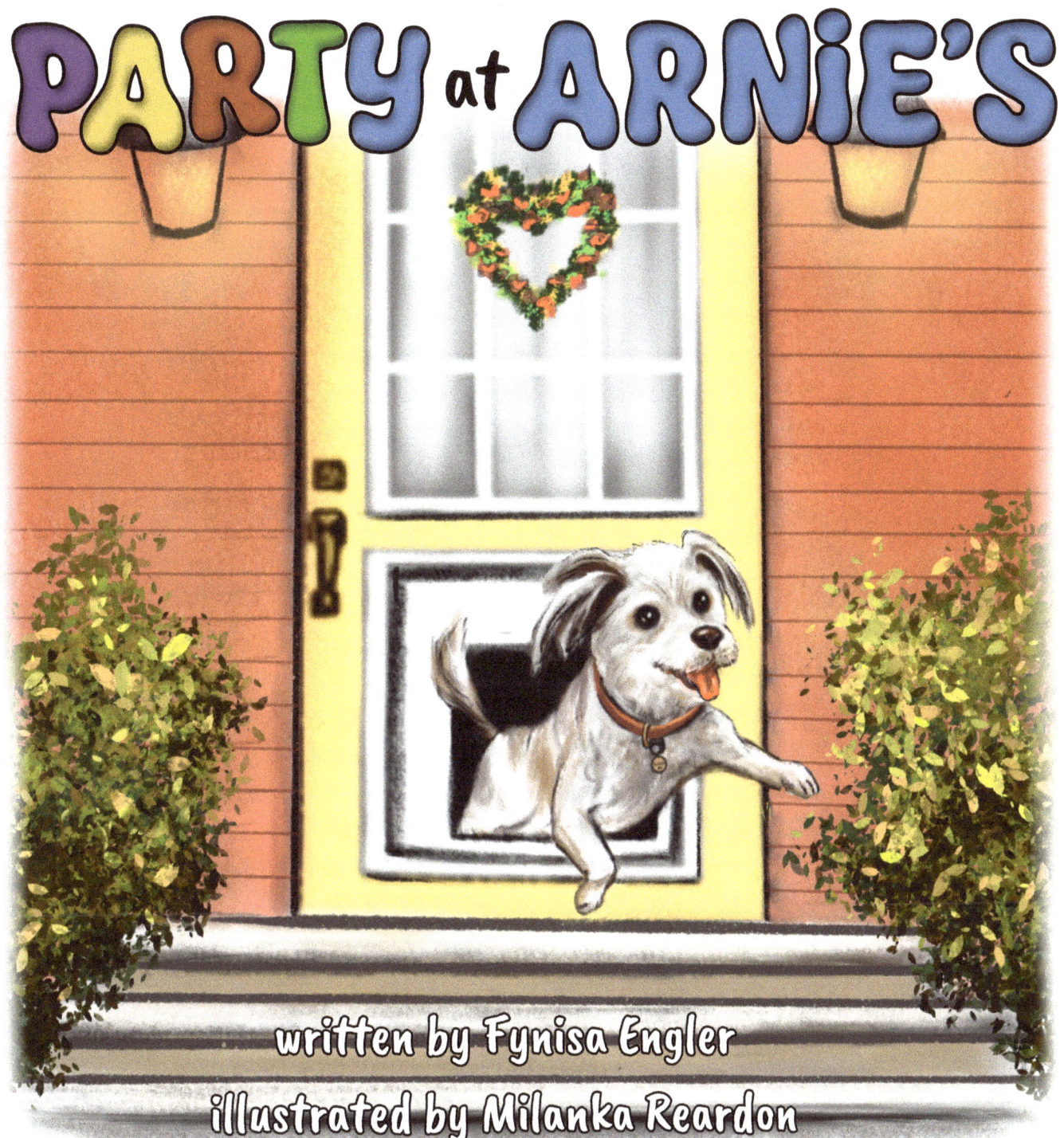

This edition first published in 2024
by Lawley Publishing,
a division of Lawley Enterprises LLC
Text Copyright © 2024 by Fynisa Engler
Illustration Copyright © 2024 by Milanka Reardon
All Rights Reserved

Hardcover ISBN 978-1-960137-04-3
Paperback ISBN 978-1-960137-06-7
Library of Congress Control Number: 2023935683

Lawley Publishing
70 S. Val Vista Dr. #A3 #188
Gilbert, AZ 85296
LawleyPublishing.com

To my husband and daughter, and of course, the real-life Arnie. —FE

*To Leo, Catalina, and sweet baby.
And also to Clover, Winnie, and Snowball.* —MR

Arnie watched as his best friend, Lucy, pulled out of the driveway.
"It's time!" he exclaimed, jumping off the couch.
He ran out his doggy door to the backyard.

"IT'S TIME," he barked. "PARTY TIME!"
"Party at Arnie's," all the neighborhood dogs barked.

"Party at Arnie's?" Stanley the Squirrel asked, poking his head out of a tree. What's a party? he wondered.

Soon Arnie's house was full of dogs of all sizes.
There was Spike the Bulldog, Chi Chi the shivering Chihuahua,
and even the badly behaved Rufus who lived up the street.

Dogs danced on the tables as the music played.

Stanley peered in the window. Wow, a party looks like fun.
He crept over to the doggy door and waited for the perfect moment to sneak in.

Suddenly, a huge, furry dog ran past.
"Here's my chance." Stanley jumped on
the dog's back without him noticing.

And just like that, Stanley was in the house.
"WOW, Chester, your tail is looking extra fluffy today," Spike said with a mouth full of food. "Arnie, these hotdogs are delicious."

"PEE-YEW Spike, you STINK," Arnie said, holding his nose.
"Oops, I think I ate too much," Spike laughed, embarrassed.
Stanley thought he was going to faint from the awful smell.

Suddenly, Arnie heard someone yell, "WEE!"
He turned around just as Rufus swung by on the chandelier.
"Rufus, get down! You're going to break it!" Arnie yelled.

"How do I get down from here?" Rufus called, swinging back and forth. Finally, he let go and landed on the table with a big thud. Stanley scurried for cover.

"Arnie," a small voice called.
Arnie looked down and saw Chi Chi staring up at him, shivering.
"What's up, Chi Chi?"
"So, I got scared on the carpet. And you know what happens when I get scared."

"OH NO! You peed on the carpet?" Arnie panicked.
"Sorry."
Arnie grabbed a blanket and scrubbed and scrubbed.
Even I know to pee outside, Stanley thought.

Just as Arnie was enjoying the party again, dirt landed on his head. He looked up to see Spike digging in Lucy's favorite plant. "Spike, stop!" yelled Arnie.

"What? Oh, sorry, I was trying to find a spot to hide my bone," said Spike.

"Hey Arnie, sorry to bother you, but Rufus is in the bathroom making a huge mess."
Arnie rushed to the bathroom. There was Rufus with his head in the toilet.
"Toilet water is so good," Rufus barked as water splashed all over the bathroom floor.

"RUFUS, water bowl buddy. DRINK ONLY FROM THE WATER BOWL!"

Arnie quickly wiped up the toilet water.

Once Arnie left, Stanley was very curious about the bathroom. What's toilet water? he wondered, taking a taste.

"YUCK!" he exclaimed, trying to wipe the taste from his tongue.

Just then, Spike ran in from outside. "Arnie, I just heard Fritz from five blocks over barking," he said. "He just saw Lucy drive past his house. **SHE'S COMING HOME!**"

"Oh no," Arnie panicked. **"PARTY'S OVER, PARTY'S OVER,"** he barked.

All the dogs rushed out the doggy door, leaving behind a gigantic mess.

Stanley hurried to the doggy door,
but it was too heavy for him to open.

Arnie ran as fast as he could around the house, trying to clean up the mess.

Stanley ran as fast as he could around the house, trying to find a way out.

I'm never going to finish in time, Arnie thought.

I'm never going to get out in time, Stanley thought.

"Arnie," Lucy called as she opened the front door. "I came home early so you wouldn't be lonely. Oh my goodness, what happened here?" she exclaimed.

Immediately, Stanley spotted the open door and made a run for it.

"Squirrel!" Lucy yelled.

"Squirrel!" Arnie barked as Stanley ran out the front door.

"Oh, Arnie, you must have been so scared while that squirrel made this huge mess. You poor boy," Lucy said, hugging Arnie.

Meet the real-life Arnie. Arnie is named after the legendary golfer Arnold Palmer. Sandy and Leslie adopted Arnie from an animal rescue in Santa Rosa, CA, on New Year's Day in 2016. They knew he would be part of their family as soon as they saw him. Now Arnie enjoys living in sunny Arizona. When he's not planning his next party, he enjoys going for walks, rides in the car, and sunbathing. Arnie loves everyone, and he hopes you enjoyed *Party at Arnie's*.

Fynisa Engler takes her love of writing children's books and combines it with her imagination of what crazy things pets do when their owners are away. Fynisa lives in sunny Arizona with her husband, daughter, and three dogs named Belle, Lily, and Molly. She loves traveling and spending time with family and friends. She even enjoys Mondays because that's when she gets to work with her wonderful writing group!

Milanka Reardon began illustrating at a young age. When she emigrated to the U.S. from the former Republic of Yugoslavia at the age of six, no one in her school spoke her language, so her teachers sketched images of English words for her. Instead of copying the words, Milanka took it upon herself to add to their drawings, creating her first stories with images. Later, she attended the Rhode Island School of Design, earning certificates in children's book illustration and natural science illustration. She is a recipient of the R. Michelson Galleries Emerging Artist Award. She lives in Massachusetts by a lake, where she loves to sketch her favorite dogs as well as swans, ducks, and other wildlife. You can see some of her artwork on her website at MilankaReardon.com.

Printed in the USA
CPSIA information can be obtained
at www.ICGtesting.com
LVHW061452210124
769470LV00014B/278